THE PIZZA PLACE GHOST

Written by Class 1-208
Illustrated by Duendes del Sur

Hello Reader — Level 1

ISBN 0-439-20495-X

23   40   12 13/0

Designed by Mary Hall

Printed in the U.S.A.

First Scholastic printing, November 2000

SCHOLASTIC INC.

New York Toronto London Auckland Sydney
Mexico City New Delhi Hong Kong

One day, was reading the

 .

"Listen to this," she said to ,

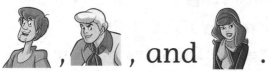 , and .

"All the is missing from

Frank's Place."

" ? ?" said. "Like,

I want to eat! Let's go to Frank's

 Place!"

At the place, and his

friends sat down at a .

Frank told them the story.

"At the end of the day, a

comes and brings me ,"

Frank said.

"But when I come in the next

day, the is always gone!

And I cannot make without

 !"

"I do not know what happens to the  ," Frank said.

"Every night I put the away. Then I close all the . I put a big on the . No one can get in."

"No one but a !" said.

"Ruh-roh!" said . He hid under a .

"We need to look for clues," 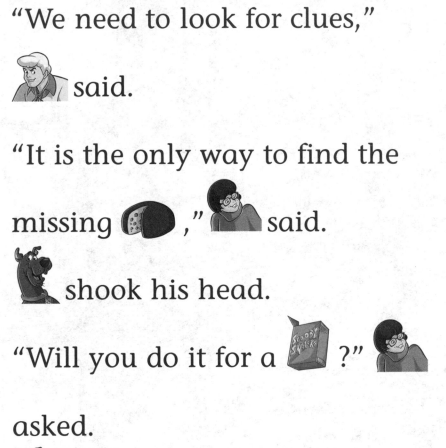 said.

"It is the only way to find the missing ," said.

shook his head.

"Will you do it for a ?"

asked.

jumped up.

"Let's split up," 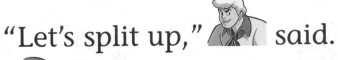 said.

 went into the kitchen.

"Like, I want something to eat,"

he said.

 took out some .

He took out a bag of .

He took out some .

He made a big mess.

" ... !" said.

followed the .

He bumped into .

"Look!" said . "A trail of ."

and followed the

and the trail of .

and bumped into .

"Look!" said . "A trail of

."

, , and followed the

, the trail of , and the

trail of .

The clues led them to the

kitchen.

"What are you doing,  ?!"

said  ,  , and  .

 turned red. "I wanted

something to eat," he said.

"Where is  ?"  asked.

 did not know.

 was missing, too.

The gang went to look for  .

The gang found 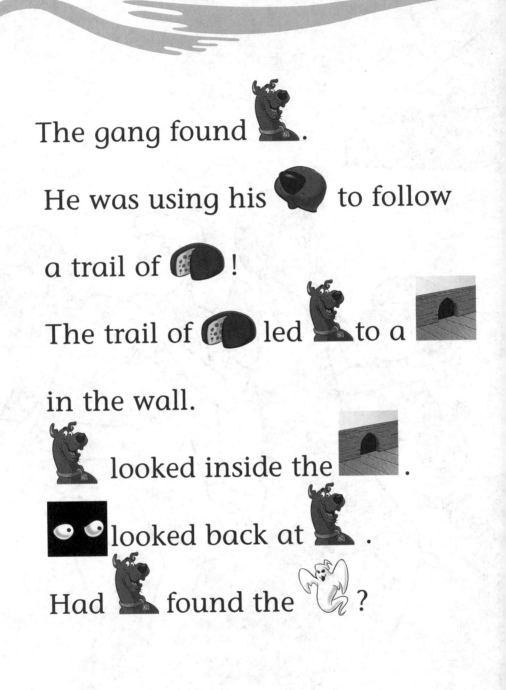.

He was using his 🦴 to follow

a trail of 🧀 !

The trail of 🧀 led 🐕 to a 🕳

in the wall.

🐕 looked inside the 🕳 .

👀 looked back at 🐕 .

Had 🐕 found the 👻 ?

put his paw into the  .

And what did he find?

 ! The had taken the

 !

Frank was happy. Now he could

make  .

And he made the biggest  for

 and his friends!

CHEESE FOUND!

Did you spot all the picture clues in this Scooby-Doo mystery?

Each picture clue is on a flash card. Ask a grown-up to cut out the flash cards. Then try reading the words on the back of the cards. The pictures will be your clue.

Reading is fun with Scooby-Doo!

newspaper	Velma
Shaggy	Scooby
Daphne	Fred

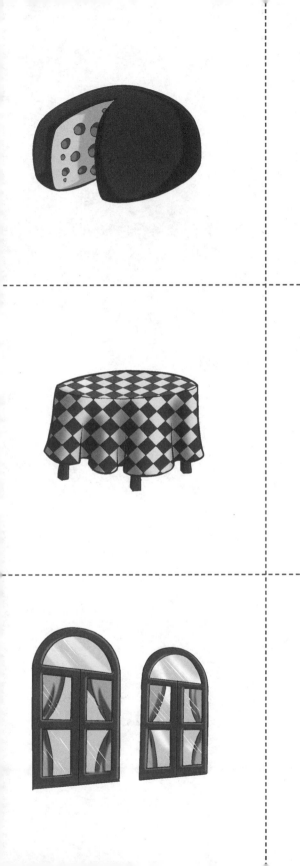

pizza	cheese
truck	table
lock	windows

ghost	door
Scooby Snacks	chair
flour	tomatoes

footprints	pepperoni
hole	nose
mice	eyes